A Poetry Journey: Echoes from the Past

H-R Watts

Copyright © 2026 H-R Watts

All rights reserved.

ISBN: 978-1-0369-5076-7

CONTENTS

ACKNOWLEDGEMENT

With gratitude to the historic places of Britain... especially Bletchley Park, whose quiet corridors and enduring legacy stirred the heart of this collection.

Though the women in these verses are fictional, they are written in honour of those whose lives, work, and hidden loves may never have been recorded, yet whose presence shaped history in ways we still feel today.

This collection speaks for the unspoken and is offered with deep respect to those whose truths were lived quietly, bravely, and often unseen.

AUTHOR NOTE

Welcome and thank you for choosing to walk beside me through these pages of history.

Thank you for sharing in the quiet loves and tender echoes of the women who lived in the shadows of wartime Britain.

If any of these poems stay with you for a while, or bring a moment of tenderness, I would be grateful if you shared your thoughts in a review on Amazon and/or Goodreads.

Your voice helps new readers discover mine, and together we keep these stories alive.

The front cover photograph is the property of Helen-Robin Watts ©2025

Love & Light,
H-R Watts

www.h-r-watts.com

A Secret Echo

As I sit by the lake lost in thought

I watch the gentle ripples of the water

hearing the trees swaying softly in the autumn breeze

as I look up across the lake, I see her sitting on the memorial bench

her gaze appears to drift as though her thoughts lie somewhere else

I wonder, *what is she thinking*, her expression is indescribable

she has a kind of seriousness that I cannot quite pin down

I look at the way her brown subtle wavy hair gently moves with the breeze

I notice she is wearing a brown dress, finished with a worn leather belt

then, as though she senses me, she looks up across the water in my direction

my breath hitches, I find I cannot look away for being obvious that I should stare

to my surprise, she smiles at me, a delicate smile and I cannot help but return that smile our gaze upon each other holds for a moment longer

before her beautiful form disappears before me

my smile falters as I realise, she is no longer there

just an empty bench and the sound of bustling visitors
adorn the grounds

and the beautiful woman from the nineteen forties, is
nowhere to be seen.

Lakeside Attraction

Olive walks the gravel track around the lake

as she comes to an empty wooden bench, she sits quietly

she opens her tin tuck box and unwraps her sandwich

the rustling of the wax paper against the silence of the lake

It's two forty-two in the afternoon and she is late to eat lunch again, working that last code was challenging

the smell of the egg and cress sandwich engulfs her nostrils

"Mmm" she murmurs "so glad my grandmother has chickens" she smiles appreciatively at the small luxury

eggs are rare; however, her grandmother's chickens laid about five eggs a week

she sits gazing out over the silent lake, watching the subtle ripples on the surface of the water

appreciating this moment without the chaos of the hut… with endless messages piling up on the centre desk

lunch and peace were just what Olive needed.

Lost in her own head, her thoughts were interrupted by the sound of a throat clearing

Olive looks up to see the most incredible and beautiful woman in a WREN's uniform… she has short blonde tight curls, a wide smile and piercing blue eyes

the woman begins to speak, "Your Sandwich smells delightful, is that egg?"

Olive chuckles forgetting for a moment how rare eggs are in general

"It's egg and cress that my grandmother made for me… I live with her you see" Olive follows her words with a shy smile crossing her lips, her brown hair with subtle waves rest upon her shoulders as she gazes up at the beautiful woman before her

a moment of silence and the WREN opens her mouth to speak "Would you mind so much if one can join you?" she indicates to the bench

Olive who is usually shy holds her gaze, her lips curve slightly before replying, "Please do, it would be lovely to have company" she watches as the blonde woman takes a seat close to her

their thighs gently touching, Olive feels a frisson through her body, a blush creeps across her cheeks as the woman looks at her with side eye

to disperse the awkward moment between them Olive asks, "Would you like the other half of my sandwich?" she holds up the tin box the stranger now grinning widely at the offer "I would love it… if, you are sure?"

Olive nods her head as the woman excitedly retrieves the half sandwich, taking a bite with an appreciative moan

Olive chuckles *that moan certainly made her realise her own body is working just fine*

"What?" the blonde asks "this is so delicious… your grandmother is a sandwich genius"

Olive blushes again and dips her head "I'm glad you like it, and I will let my grandmother know you approve" she pauses "I'm Olive by the way"

the woman stops mid-chew to gaze into Olive's eyes "I'm Elizabeth, and it's a real pleasure to meet you Olive" she extends her hand

Olive takes her hand in a gentle shake, as she embraces her body's reaction to the soft touch of Elizabeth's hand in hers

they both continue looking out over the calm of the lake, with no words, just pure appreciation for quiet and for each other.

Love in the Skies

Joyce sits alone in the mess hall sipping tea

she closes her eyes, tuning in to the surrounding sounds

... officers talking, laughing and fleeting conversations

as she opens her eyes and looks out of the window

the once dense fog, now lifting from over the airfield

a crackle from the Tannoy, followed by the soft Scottish voice that spoke:

"All pilots report to the operations room please."

she smiles as she listens to the voice...

... a voice that made her feel warm and safe inside

she stands ready in her flight jumpsuit, grabs her parachute pack, helmet and goggles

she starts making her way across the grounds to the ops room and airfield.

Taking the iron steps up, she joins the queue of pilots

the butterflies evident in her stomach as she gets closer to the hatch...

then a soft voice interrupts her thoughts:

"Morning Joyce, how are ye this morning?"

she gazes at the woman on the other side…

with fiery red shoulder length curls, and a smile to melt a thousand hearts

Joyce replies: "Morning Edith, I'm good thanks. What you got for me today?"

Edith hands her today's chit sheet, their fingers lightly touch in the exchange

an apparent frisson passes through Joyce's core followed by a deep intake of breath "Brilliant, an Ox-box and a pickup of a Mark Nine. Thanks Edith" she follows her words with a subtle wink, a wide smile and she retreats from the hatch and down the opposite stairs to the airfield

with a spring in her step, and wonderful thoughts of Edith

and *'Oh'* how she would love to run her fingers through those delicate curls

she climbs into the cockpit, familiarises herself with the basic manual and controls

then she confidently starts the engine and makes her way to the runway.

Minutes later she is climbing the clouds, before finalising her stats

the quiet brings a moment of reflection to the one she truly loves

"Oh Edith.... how I long for a kiss from your lips" she mumbles

with a shy smile she continues her journey through the skies

the only place she can fully acknowledge her love for another

and not be judged.

Melting Hearts

It was day one for Ella in the office at the munitions factory

she steps through the open double doors to be met by the most mesmerising person

"Y'alright love? I'm Bobbie, can I 'elp ya?"

Bobbie holds her hand out; all smudged with grease and with brazen confidence

Ella stares into those dark brown eyes; to be polite she takes Bobbie's hand

secretly melting inside at that thick Yorkshire accent

"I-I'm Ella," she stammers, "I'm starting work here today"

she speaks softly, shyly, nervously, a moment stretched like a lifetime

gazing curiously into each other's eyes Ella's thoughts come forth

Oh, that handshake, so strong but soft to the touch

she takes a deep breath, a curve of her lips giving her away

reluctantly she lets go of Bobbie's hand

"I should go… I don't want to be late" Ella says and turns

on her heel and begins to ascend the iron staircase to the office

her heart pounding, heels clacking against metal steps

warmth rising within her and something else… she can't explain

reaching the top of the staircase, she glances over her shoulder

and there she sees Bobbie with those eyes of dark pools, a cute smile and confident nature looking back up at her with a wide grin

Ella quietly giggles, and blushes profusely before returning the smile

she then sends a shy wave Bobbie's way, before entering the office to start her first day.

To Love Silently

Jean stands leaning casually against the front of her Bedford truck

enjoying the fresh air whilst waiting for her pickup to land

this wasn't just any pickup, this was Betty… the sweet, chatty ferry pilot

Jean smiles subtly at herself, the thought of Betty's non-stop talking

she loves the sound of Betty's enthusiastic chattering voice

there was something quite sensational about the woman

her thoughts were then interrupted by the too familiar sound of wolf whistles coming from the airfield groundsmen

looking up she spots the curvaceous Betty in her subtly creased flying suit, carrying her parachute pack, helmet and goggles

Betty, not paying mind to whistles, waves and smiles enthusiastically at Jean

My god that smile, and them bouncing mouse brown curls
Jean's thoughts escape her

"Hey stranger." Betty says as she bumps Jean's hip with

hers

Jean laughs, "Hey yourself, how was the flight today?"

Betty climbs into the truck along with Jean

"Oh, you know… minimal tools, maximum common sense and all that Jazz" Betty chuckles

Jean starts the engine and pulls away before replying

"I don't know how you girls do it, climb into a cockpit not knowing what might happen up there. I'm glad you're safe though" she smiles sympathetically

Betty switches on the portable radio and sighs happily as she hears her favourite song

and boy does Jean know what's coming next

Betty belts out *White Cliffs of Dover*, the pure silkiness in her voice, then hitting them high notes with ease

Jean turns to her grinning and chuckling encouragingly

she really does enjoy this side of Betty who lets her hair down after a flight.

A few minutes pass and Betty stops singing "You got any plans tonight, Jeanie?"

Jean melts inside at the nickname she has grown

accustomed to, shaking her head she replies, "No plans... why do you ask?"

Betty with that glint in her eye and that sweet smile... the kind of smile like butter wouldn't melt "Well I was thinking... as my landlady is out tonight, and we have left over veggie stew" she pauses before continuing "would you like to join me for dinner tonight?" her eyebrows quirk up in anticipation of the answer

Jean stares for a moment, a slight curve to her lips before replying "I'd love to come to dinner, and I'll bring some wine my dad brought back from France"

Betty perks up, sitting up straight and enthusiastically, with a slight bounce in her seat at the acceptance

Jean continues with a knowing smile "Shall I bring anything else?"

with that Betty smirks and replies in her most cheerful tone "Nope, just the wine and more importantly... your beautiful self," she winks teasingly

Jean's heart flutters... her face flushed as she acknowledges "Great I'll be there" she pauses momentarily before asking "any particular time?"

Betty excitedly replies, "Seven-thirty suit you?"

Jean nods in agreement, with a contented smile as they continue their journey.

Threads of Love

The textile factory opens at seven in the morning;
Monique arrives ready for her day

she heads for the tea trolley and makes a cuppa before the day starts

her lips curve into an almost smile as she hears familiar footsteps echoing down the hall

in walks Dottie, with her dirty blonde cropped hair and that killer smile, and radiating pure joy for a Monday morning

Monique pretends not to notice until she hears that cockney twang, although a very sweet voice

"'Ello Mon, d'ya have good weekend"

looking up from the drinks trolley, with a knowing smirk on her face Monique replies, "It was beautiful mon trésor, and you?"

Dottie grins widely and practically bouncing on her heels "Well, I got a new book, and it was" she pauses for a moment "beautiful, I felt alive just reading it"

Monique stares curiously at her "You have me intrigued ma chérie"

Monique then pours a cup of tea with a dash of milk, and

one sugar and hands it to Dottie

Dottie takes the cup with an appreciative smile "Fanks Mon, you're a star"

they both continue idle chat until just before seven-thirty rolls around and work starts

Monique can't help but be drawn to Dottie and thinking about *her hair… her smile that could stop a production line, and those dark eyes so deeply entrancing*

they both sit at their workstations, sewing machines at the ready

the floor manager switches on the radio and Monique knows that today is going to be a fabulous day

then the women get to work… the sound of the machine's steady, soothing thudding

then the beautiful sound of Dottie humming along to the radio as the music unfolds

Monique's lips curve into a mischievous smile, as she has waited the whole weekend for this very moment, sitting in the same room as Dottie

Deep in thought of t*he woman she is deeply in love with and has been since all those months ago.*

Love by the Lakeside

Elizabeth sits quietly next to Olive, the comfortable silence allowing her time to finish her half of the sandwich Olive gave her

the distinct taste of egg, salad cream and cress satisfies her tastebuds

she smiles to herself, this woman next to her was… so profoundly beautiful in heart, mind and soul

she was the first to break the silence. "I work over in hut 11 with the Bombe machines" Elizabeth pauses before continuing "I don't think I've seen you around… I would have definitely remembered you if I had" a meaningful smile crosses her lips

Olive turns to face her, the tin tuck box slightly moving in her lap, the sound of the metal lid under the open box disturbs the silence momentarily

"I work in hut 6… I usually take my lunch late and normally arrive before the others do. I like to savour the moment of peace in the hut before the chaos starts and I am always the last to leave" Olive says with a hesitant smile

Elizabeth observes Olive closely with a curious eye "That will explain why I haven't seen you before then."

a momentary silence falls between them

Elizabeth continues "I usually get here before my start time, and I am usually at the main house for lunch… their mince and potatoes are an absolute luxury when it's on the menu. Today though, I needed a break, my ears are ringing terribly from the machines" she follows her words with a wry smile

they sit; gazes locked onto each other… the silence comfortable… the chemistry palpable

Olive's mouth slightly agape in hesitation of delivering words, the calm water rippling from the lake is an appreciative distraction

Olive speaks "What are you doing this Sunday morning?" her hands are shaking nervously as she asks

Elizabeth reaches out with her hands, covering Olive's and giving a reassuring smile "I have nothing going on this weekend… what did you have in mind?"

"Well… I usually take an early morning walk on Sundays in the countryside and then head home for lunch" Olive pauses… she is hesitant but calm with Elizabeth's hands on hers, she continues "I-I was wondering…" she stammers nervously

Elizabeth noticing Olive's nerves gently chimes in "I would love to join you on your walk" she squeezes Olive's hands and gives her a cheeky wink immediately Olive feels the nerves disperse, "Would you like to come to mine and my grandmother's for Sunday lunch too?" one eyebrow raised in anticipation

Elizabeth grins with excitement, trying to contain herself "Well if your grandmother's sandwiches are anything to go by then her Sunday lunch might actually kill me" she chuckles "Count me in Olive… I would be honoured to come for lunch this Sunday and more honoured to accompany you on your walk"

Elizabeth smiles softly before turning her gaze back to the lake

Olive's excitement is building inside, and a slight squeak passes her lips as she tries to suppress it

Elizabeth chuckles softly at the noise from Olive, understanding the same excitement

as they both look out over the calm water and gentle ripples for the remaining few minutes

they hadn't realised how subconsciously, they had linked pinkie fingers on the bench

their discreet way of showing each other affection, even though they have just met.

Hidden Love at the Base

Edith shuffles the chit sheets ready to hand out

then she spots the name… that name… the only name that races through her mind

her thoughts playing through her head *Joyce, if only you knew*

Edith opens the hatch ready to distribute crates to the pilots

for each passing pilot, she anticipates the arrival of Joyce

her heart pounding, her stomach lined with butterflies, like a kind of nervousness, but also excitement

the moment disperses as the next pilot is not whom she wants it to be

her thoughts racing again *what a wee adorable lass she is*

then, as she is lost within her own thoughts, it's as though she manifests the one she loves

Joyce stands there before her… she gently greets her a good morning

her legs discretely trembling behind the hatch counter, her inner thoughts consuming her O*h my… those blue eyes, that wee wide smile, that gorgeous brown hair with soft waves* she shakes her head momentarily before handing the chit sheet over, their fingers touch gently, and she feels the reaction deep within her core

Joyce appears to be happy with her crates today

Edith goes to speak… the knowing of the queue behind Joyce, she knows she cannot ask her question now

she improvises and says, "Have a safe flight!" she follows her words with a concerned smile

Joyce replies softly "Thanks… I'll see you later" with a nod of her head and retreating footsteps she is gone

Edith sighs with a silent disappointment, making a mental note to meet with Joyce

her thoughts are disrupted by the face of the next pilot

she sifts through the chit sheets and hands it over with a friendly smile, as she goes about her daily duties.

Love in Motion

Bobbie is undertaking her work on the munitions factory floor

today she was tasked with making the Copper bands in shell casings

as she works, she can't get the new girl out of her head

those baby blues, silky red shoulder length victory curls and that shy smile... and when she blushed it was the cutest thing

Bobbie softly smiles at the thoughts emanating in her mind

she knows she must concentrate; anything could go wrong if she loses focus

but *My god, Ella and that cute stammer* she smirks to herself

her inner voice screaming *Stop it Bobbie! You can't afford for anything to go wrong*

as time passes, she hears the siren, indicating lunch break

Bobbie goes and retrieves her tuck box from her locker and heads outside

she bends down to sit on the loading dock, her legs dangling

the strong scent of tobacco from the nearby smokers hits her nostrils she closes her eyes as she takes a bite from her cucumber sandwich, it has a sprinkle of salt to counteract the bland taste

"Cucumber sandwiches, the story of my life" she mumbles

the moment interrupted by a familiar voice from behind her

"Bobbie… isn't it?"

Bobbie looks behind and upward, and sees that smile that has been on her mind all morning… she stands up "Aye… that's me" she grins with excitement

Ella gazes into her eyes before speaking "So… do you live around here?" she looks on in anticipation of the reply

Bobbie coughs as she swallows a bit of her sandwich "Sorry… tha' went down the wrong 'ole" she clears her throat before speaking again "aye, I live abou' five minutes from 'ere, across the park" she pauses "what abou' you love?"

Ella smiles, enjoying being called 'love' in that Yorkshire accent, "I live across the park too, I rent a room in a boarding house with a few other girls"

There's that cute blush again Bobbie thinks to herself whilst smirking

"Well…" Bobbie begins "if you finish the same time as me, maybe we can walk 'ome together, it's usually dark around the time I leave so I'd be stoked for company" she gazes at Ella with hopeful eyes

Ella grins

Mmmmm is that a glint in her eye Bobbie thinks to herself

"I'd really like that." Ella says her lips curve into a satisfied smile "shall we meet in the locker room"

Bobbie excitedly replies "Aye love… meet you in the locker room around six" she pauses before continuing "I do usually shower before I 'ead 'ome so… it might be around quarter past six before I'm ready"

Ella blushes at the thought of Bobbie just out of the shower "That's fine… I'm happy to wait for you" she nods and smiles, then turns to walk away

Bobbie calls after her "I'll see ya la'er then love" she chuckles

Ella calls back "You will" and she disappears

Bobbie checks her grandfather's pocket watch, and heads back to her locker and places her tuck box inside

"Wow… she is one 'ell of a gorgeous woman" she mutters as she heads back to the factory floor.

Driving Love Home

Betty sits upon the worn, rexine seat in the Bedford

the portable radio is playing some of her favourite songs

she can smell the musty scent of the truck, mixed with stale tobacco from the fabric of Jean's uniform

she can't help but feel inner excitement after Jean accepted her invitation

and *oh boy* is she looking forward to that promised French wine

Betty has wanted to be alone with Jean for a while now, outside of their work

she just couldn't find the courage to ask

from the first time they met five months ago she was drawn to Jean with her *shoulder length black curls, warm brown complexion and those dark brown eyes.* Good no-nonsense Jean is what Betty calls her

when she sees Jean standing by her truck, smoking her usual woodbine, she can't help but smile and drift into thought *Jean… I truly believe you are the one for me*

"So, we have a bit of a way to go… do you want to stop for

a cuppa somewhere?" Jean's words interrupt Betty's thoughts

Oh, that husky voice Betty thinks before answering "Absolutely… that would be lovely" she grins widely because any excuse to spend more time with Jean is great

Jean nods as she drives through the next village as they head back down south

"You, okay? You seem a tad quiet" Jean says placing a concerned hand on Betty's knee

Betty takes a deep intake of breath at the touch, heat rushing through her core "Ummm, yes, I'm fine… just thinking about dinner later" she pauses a moment "I hope left over stew will be okay for you?"

Jean pulls up to the curb near the café, she switches off the engine and turns in her seat to face Betty "I love stew and it's a real treat for someone like me, I don't get to eat a hot meal often, it's always a sandwich and if I'm lucky I get a Cheese and Piccalilli one" she gives Betty a cheeky grin

Betty laughs "I'm glad to hear that, my landlady really knows how to cook, and she told me to finish the stew. I even tried my hand at baking bread" she smiles proudly with a quirk of her eyebrows

Jean chuckles "I'm intrigued Betty… now I wouldn't mind a sandwich using your bread" she winks

Betty laughs with a snort, feeling the butterflies in her stomach at Jean's words "You won't be saying that when you chip a tooth on it"

they both roll up laughing at Betty's words, and then they exit the truck and walk towards the entrance of Angela's Café

Betty linking arms with Jean, relishing the simple contact as they open the door and head inside for a 'halfway' cuppa

the scent of baked goods, and freshly brewed coffee fills her nostrils, the clatter of cups as drinks are being prepared

Jean turns to Betty "Go grab that corner table and I will get these" she smiles

Betty's heart flutters at the simple gesture with a hesitant look before replying "If, you're sure? I am happy to pay for my own or for both of us" a concerned curve to her lips appears

"Honestly, I will get these as you are preparing dinner for us later… now go grab that table before someone else does" Jean laughs and gives a cheeky wink

Betty melts at the wink "Okay" and with that she turns on her heel and heads for the table with love in her heart, and a bounce in her step.

Love Sewn Deep

Dottie walks to the front entrance of the clothing factory

It's mid-morning break, and she needs some air

as she steps outside pulling her coat together, she spots Monique having a cigarette

she admires Monique's black victory curls, her dark brown eyes and that red lipstick

"Eh Mon I was thinking…" Dottie begins with a grin

Monique, with a curious smile on her face replies "What were you thinking ma chérie?"

"Ow d'ya fancy lunch down the café today… pie and liquor are on the menu?" Dottie asks

"I think I would like that very much" Monique says with a cute smile and another puff on her cigarette

Dottie can't contain herself; she bounces on her heels… as she does a lot of the time

"Great…" Dottie pauses before continuing "my treat, I 'ave enough money for us both"

and with that Dottie turns on her heel and scurries back into the factory before Monique can protest

with a smile on her face, a flutter in her heart and knowing in just two hours she will spend an hour with the one her heart yearns for… Monique!

Back on the factory floor, the chatter quietens as break comes to an end, Monique rounds the corner

a subtle blush of pink crosses Dottie's face… she quickly dips her head down

Monique grinning as she spots the blush, she doesn't say anything out of respect, she just takes her seat back at her machine

Dottie's thoughts of *how a love so beautiful… can be so cruel.*

Love Comes to the Countryside

It's five forty-six in the morning according to Olive's watch

It's Sunday morning and she is waiting by the kissing gate for Elizabeth to arrive

Olive is wearing a long brown wool coat and her burgundy beret, with a jumper and brown corduroy trousers and wellies.

Meanwhile, Elizabeth is walking down the narrow lane toward the meeting point

she is wearing her black wool jacket and green scarf, underneath, she is wearing a jumper and an old pair of black trousers. *Oh my, it's cold out here, I should have brought my hat* she thinks to herself

enjoying the smell of the fresh damp morning air and the sky still dark, she gives out a yawn

then she spots her "Yoo-hoo... Olive" she says waving excitedly at her

"Morning Elizabeth, how are you? I do hope this isn't too early for you" Olive speaks noticing Elizabeth looking a little tired as she searches her gaze curiously

Elizabeth playfully waves her off "Not at all… I wouldn't miss this walk for all the tea in China" she says with a slight curve to the corner of her lips

Olive opens the kissing gate as Elizabeth follows her through, without waiting her turn… the closeness of their bodies sending both their hearts racing

Olive's thoughts running wild *I love how she feels against me* she bites her lower lip out of sight of Elizabeth

they both pass through the gate as they make their way up the muddy countryside track, with fields on the right, and trees on the left of them

the fresh damp air sticks to their cheeks, and the silence is deafening

"So… how was your Saturday" Elizabeth asks, breaking the silence

Olive replies with a tender smile "I didn't really do much. I went to the local shop to get the weekly allowance of meat… it's what we are having today. Unfortunately, my grandmother has issues with her legs so she can't really walk more than about five minutes"

their shoulders touch as they walk and chat, Olive's body feeling more alive than ever

"You know… if you, or your grandmother should ever need a lift anywhere or just a run out, I do have a car"

Elizabeth pauses looking slightly to her right at Olive as she speaks

"Really... you wouldn't mind?" Olive asks with a slight apprehension

Elizabeth grins, sensing Olive's discomfort with accepting her offer, she loops her arm through Olive's "I wouldn't mind at all, the car hardly gets used as I cycle to work, so you would be doing me a favour by keeping it ticking over" she follows her words with a reassuring smile and a squeeze to Olive's arm

"W-well that would be lovely, if it's really no trouble" Olive says "You see my grandmother, I do worry about her, she really wants to visit my grandfather's grave however, it's too far for her to go, we would need to get a bus to the cemetery. I catch her crying regularly staring at my grandfather's picture, unfortunately I don't drive, and she hasn't visited in over a year" Olive shyly bows her head

they continue walking along the track, and they come to a bend at the top of the hill

a log bench is nestled between the trees

"Here… let's sit" Elizabeth gestures to the bench

they both take a seat, as their hands grip the bench either side of them, they lean slightly forward

Elizabeth takes a deep breath as she feels Olive's pinkie finger settle next to her own

"I would be more than happy to take you and your grandmother to the cemetery; it would be an honour... we... could even take some flowers" Elizabeth offers cautiously

Olive swallows hard "Thank you... I'd like that, and it means a lot to me that you would do that" she casually places her pinkie finger over Elizabeth's

Elizabeth's breath hitches again as she feels her whole body responding to such a small gesture, she turns and looks at Olive

Olive's eyes gazing back at her, full of want, it was like Elizabeth was seeing deep inside her soul and connecting, she can't stop the words from tripping over her lips "I... I really want to kiss you Olive" tears pricking her eyes with fear she has overstepped, she bows her head

then as though something takes over Olive, she raises her hand and turns Elizabeth's face to look at her own, she speaks softly, quietly... a whisper even "I want to kiss you too, so badly... since the first time we met on that bench"

with Olive's words, so unexpected, tears trickle down Elizabeth's face

Olive frowns, and then cups Elizabeth's face with both her hands, wiping the tears away with her thumb-pads a moment of pure silence, bar the morning song from the birds in the surrounding trees

the sun slowly rising above the fields in the distance

with that, they lean into each other, feeling warm breath against their skin, then their lips softly touch

a small moan escapes Olive's lips against the kiss… the deepening kiss becoming more intense

Olive's fingers and hands still cupping Elizabeth's tearstained cheeks

Elizabeth wraps her arms around Olive's waist pulling her closer

reluctantly, they then pull away, faces flushed pink… or was it just the cold, their eyes meet momentarily, and a slight smile appears upon their faces

the moment of no words spoken, says everything they need to say

the sun now fully rising and suddenly, a break in their silence as a couple walk over the brow of the hill

"Good morning" the couple speak cheerily as they hold hands passing by them

"Morning" Olive and Elizabeth say in unison followed by a mischievous giggle as the couple are unaware of what just happened a couple of minutes ago then Olive says, "Shall we head back to mine now… I can show you the chickens who laid the egg you ate half of the other day" she smirks before continuing "and I will need to help my grandmother make lunch"

Elizabeth grins widely "You are so damn adorable Olive" she steals another quick peck from Olive's lips then rises "Come on then, let's get back to yours and see these chucks, and I will help with lunch too" she holds her arm out to Olive

Olive stands and loops her arm through Elizabeth's and they head back down the track towards home.

Heart in Flight

Joyce steps out of the locker room where she keeps her parachute pack, helmet and goggles

she heads toward the mess hall and accommodations

as she steps through the double doors, the scent of mince and potatoes coming from the canteen hits her nostrils

Joyce closes her eyes just for a moment

then a voice interrupts her thoughts… a familiar voice

"Hello Joyce, ye back just noo?" Edith smiles, feeling a flutter in her heart

Joyce returns the smile as she opens her eyes "Edith, how are you? And yes, I am just back now. Have you eaten?"

Edith's face flushes pink, she cannot help her reaction around Joyce

"Aye… just had mince and tatties" she follows her words with a chuckle

Joyce smiles, stepping closer to Edith, with slight caution, "I was wondering if you'd like to join me for a drink in my room, it's been a long day and I'd appreciate some company… you know how some of the ground crew are at airfields, they're not one for chatting with us female pilots" she raises her eyebrows in anticipation

Joyce feels nervous asking; she has wanted to ask Edith for the longest time to have a drink with her

Edith gazes at her… a smile forming on her lips, she hesitates before taking a large breath "Are ye sure ye not tired Joyce?" Edith asks with instant regret hoping Joyce doesn't say she is tired.

Edith has been meaning to ask Joyce for her company for a long time

Joyce subtly laughs to not make Edith feel uncomfortable "Of course I'm sure, I'd love your company" she gestures toward the door

they both walk to the accommodation block in idle chatter about their day, and looking forward to the weekend off

Joyce holds open the main door for Edith who steps inside first "Thank you" Edith says

smiling widely and with a flutter in her stomach Joyce replies "You're welcome, and thank you for coming"

opening the door to her room they both step inside

"Is whiskey okay?" Joyce asks as she knows that is all she has

Edith remembering she always stole her father's best whiskey when she was younger

"Aye Joyce, that would be grand" Edith says with a confident smile

Joyce pours two glasses of whiskey, her thoughts racing *I love this woman, but it would be so wrong to tell her*

she hands a glass to Edith

Edith takes the whiskey with a reassuring smile, she pats the bed next to her

"Come sit." Edith speaks and doesn't take her eyes off Joyce

they sit, sipping whiskey, then Edith shuffles closer so their thighs are lightly touching

the contact sends a frisson through Joyce's core, feeling the heat she inhales deeply

that's when Edith knows in her heart Joyce feels this too

Joyce looks to Edith "Sorry" she speaks the words softly to apologise for her noticeable breath intake

Edith looks at her "Ye don't need to apologise Joyce" she pauses searching Joyce's eyes

in a low toned voice Edith continues "I feel it too"

Joyce is taken aback, did Edith mean what Joyce thinks she meant, she swallows hard

taking Edith's glass and her own and placing them on the

floor

"Do you mean what I think you mean Edith?" she gently and cautiously tucks a bit of loose hair behind Edith's ear

Edith nods… lost for words she places her hand over Joyce's hand and cups it to her own cheek

"Aye sweetheart… I have wanted this moment for the longest time" Edith replies softly with an uncertain smile

were they on the same page with this conversation

Joyce's heart now beating faster at the words, pounding in her chest, her tongue running across her own lips

was this happening and before Joyce knew it, Edith placed her lips on hers

Edith felt a sudden jolt between her legs as her tongue met Joyce's, her stomach doing somersaults

Joyce's heart racing… her breath getting shallow with the deepening kiss

Edith moans…

Joyce's stomach alive with butterflies, and she could feel the pulsating between her own legs

they reluctantly pulled apart foreheads touching

"If I had known you felt this way too, we could have kissed sooner" Edith spoke in a soft whisper

Joyce replies in breathy tone "I know… but how could we have been sure"

they both knew she was right, neither could have known for sure what the other felt

all they know now is they didn't want this to end

Edith bites her lip nervously "That kiss Joyce…" she pauses "was worth the wait and everything more"

Joyce smiles and blushes profusely, leaning down picking up their glasses

no more words spoken, just sensual gazes over the rim of the whiskey glasses that speak a thousand words

they finally have succumbed to their feelings

hearts in flight… and a quiet love never to be shared.

Untamed Love

Bobbie appears from the locker room showers, fresh and clean

she turns to face her locker grabbing a clean vest, shirt and jumper.

Ella steps into the room, the squeak of the door gets Bobbie's attention

"Y'all right love?" Bobbie says

just at the words passing Bobbie's lips make Ella blush, she bites her lower lip at the sight of Bobbie before her

dripping black hair, vest on and the vision of Bobbie buttoning up her fly

Ella replies with a stutter "Y-yes, I'm good thanks" her cheeks flush pink and her shy smile adorning her face

Bobbie smirks, knowing the effect she has on Ella

"I'm almost done… then we can 'ead out" Bobbie says with a grin of equal excitement

Ella gazes around… the warm steam seeping from the showers into the locker-room hazes the atmosphere

her gaze drops to Bobbie's bottom in those brown corduroy trousers clinging to her curves, then Bobbie reaches for her jacket, flashing her toned stomach

Ella smiles with a soft giggle of appreciation for the sight before her

"No rush… I don't need to get back urgently" Ella says softly

"Reet… let's get outta here" Bobbie says as they head for the door and she opens it

Ella steps out followed by Bobbie, they exit the factory building in comfortable silence

"Aye it's a bit nippy out, isn't it?" Bobbie breaks the silence

Ella smiles "It is, but I always come prepared" she says buttoning up her long wool coat and putting on her beret

Bobbie grins and steps a little closer to Ella as they walk, her wanting to feel Ella next to her is comforting

Ella's heart skips a beat at the slight touch to her upper arm

"So…'ow was your first day?" Bobbie says with curiosity

Ella suddenly feels at ease by the topic of conversation, she feels like she has known Bobbie a lot longer than she has

"It was fun" Ella pauses "a bit busy on the phone, and Harry is demanding… especially for coffee"

Bobbie laughs a husky laugh "Aye, I can imagine he is love"

Ella's heart racing at how Bobbie calls her 'love', a contented smile graces her lips.

They enter the park, the fog becoming thicker as it distorts the park lights, and the path only visible about six feet ahead of them

Bobbie feels her whole core burning with the sensation of having Ella next to her

as she listens to Ella talk, she slightly brushes the back of her hand across Ella's, giving Ella the side eye to see her reaction

there it is again… *Ella's face going a shade of pink,* a light gasp escapes Ella's lips

Bobbie observes her as Ella stares back with pure want in her eyes *but is it want or is Bobbie misunderstanding*

Ella's inner thoughts overtake her *Please hold my hand*

and as though Bobbie reads her mind she gently, and cautiously interlaces her fingers with Ella's as they walk

"This okay love?" Bobbie asks quietly

Ella nods, then follows it up with a tender whisper "Oh yes"

Bobbie smirks with confidence as they continue their walk and chat about their day

as the exit to the park draws closer, this is where they will part ways

Ella sighs "Thank you for walking back with me" she pauses and bites her lower lip "I don't quite feel ready to go yet Bobbie"

Bobbie looks down at her, then she gazes around the park

the fog thickening, and no one appears to be around

Bobbie spots a tree off to the side, she pulls Ella to where the tree is

as they hide behind it, there are bushes on one side of them, then the large oak tree is blocking the path

Bobbie gazes into Ella's eyes, anticipating her next move

gently cupping Ella's face in her hands, and assessing her eyes

Ella's breath hitches in that moment, her heart beating faster, and flushed cheeks of anticipation

Bobbie slowly moves towards her, as Ella does the same

their lips softly touch into a gentle kiss, feeling part uncertainty whilst feeling so right

the short kiss then being broken... they stare into each

other's eyes

then Ella closes the gap one more time, a deeper kiss this time

Bobbie lets a moan escape her lips, getting lost in the kiss

Ella's cheeks heating up at the sound, she pulls desperately at Bobbie's coat

the once doubt of the moment, is now confirmed this is what they both want

the moment is disturbed by footsteps approaching

they quickly separate as Bobbie peeks around the large trunk of the tree

spotting just a silhouette of a figure in the dense fog, barely visible but there, the person is exiting the park

Bobbie gazes back at Ella "Fancy walking 'ome together tomorrow" she grins widely

Ella shyly looks down at her feet before replying "I'd love that, Bobbie" she bites her lower lip again

they walk back to the path momentarily holding hands, before letting go as they exit through the park gate

Ella now touching her lips, feeling where they had just kissed

Bobbie smirks, with newfound confidence and a spring in

her step

they stop and face each other, without words they hug one another tightly

Ella whispers in the embrace "Thank you… for that kiss especially"

"Anytime Ella, and I thank ya for making my day and my year love" she grins as they part, and brushes her lips against Ella's cheek in a stolen brief kiss

then they both turn and walk their separate ways, a smile on their faces, and a momentary gaze back at one another after just four steps

Ella gives a shy wave before they continue their way home.

A Love Brimming

Seven twenty-seven in the evening and Betty hears a knock at the door

she excitedly runs to the door and opens it to see Jean before her

"Wow you look lovely in that dress" Jean says not controlling her eyes widening at the sight

Betty smiles "Thanks Jean, you don't look bad yourself, you look dapper in that blazer and trousers"

she gestures for Jean to come in, and Jean follows her to the kitchen

"Oh, here's the wine I promised to bring" Jean places it on the countertop

Betty smiles mischievously "Oh that looks so good… do you want to pour us a glass whilst I dish up?"

Jean nods "Absolutely… where do you keep the glasses and corkscrew"

excitedly and humming along to the radio Betty responds "Up there in the cupboard you'll find the glasses" she taps a drawer next to her "corkscrew is in here" she pulls the drawer open

Jean grabs the corkscrew and the glasses and begins to

open the bottle

"I want to thank you again for extending an invite to me... I know food is valuable and I am truly excited about having something warm to eat" Jean speaks from the heart

Betty gives a contented smile "My landlady has a veggie garden so we make lots of veggie stew, this needed to be eaten today, and I can't eat it all myself" she ladles stew into enamel bowls

after ladling the stew, Betty cuts some bread she made earlier and puts it in a breadbasket on the table

Jean takes a seat "I truly am grateful and this stew smells absolutely delicious, it's lovely and thick too" she spoons some up and plops it back in the bowl to prove the thickness

Betty giggles "My landlady makes the best hearty stew" she looks at Jean, her heart melting at Jean's brown eyes

Jean gives a wide smile "May I?" she gestures to the breadbasket

"Of course, help yourself... I cut it thick as it's good for dipping" she winks and grins

Jean takes a chunk of bread, and they both start to eat, she dips her bread into the thick gravy and takes a bite with an appreciative moan

"You like it?" Betty says curiously about the bread they

spoke of earlier

"Like it? I love it and look" Jean flashes her teeth "no broken teeth" she giggles

Betty playfully slaps her arm "I am glad to hear that" she smiles and takes a sip of the French red wine

"What do you think of the wine… it's a Bordeaux my dad picked up from France, he gave it to me when I went to visit them last" Jean pauses "can you believe it's been in the cellar for seven years"

Betty freezes mid-eating "Wow… really? all I know is it tastes smooth, like silk and not that bitter wine taste you get at The Boar Pub" she continues eating

they devour their meals, chatting about their day, sipping wine and passing sweet glances to one another across the table

"Well, that filled a hole… thanks Betty" Jean says with a satisfied sigh and a rub of her tummy

Betty smirks "I am glad you liked it. Shall we take the wine and sit in the parlour"

Jean nods, and they both rise, taking their glasses and sitting on the small two-seater settee

a coal fire crackling away in the room, the warmth from the fire embraces their faces

"Shall I put the lamp on" Betty asks as she stands up again

Jean looks up from the settee "No thank you… I kind of like the glow of the fire, it's cozy" she pats the seat next to her

Betty sits down next to Jean again, as they lean back, Jean rests her arm along the back of the settee

"So, how do you like flying all of them planes? do you ever get scared" Jean asks

Betty shakes her head "I feel at my freest up there in the sky, I can be who I want to be with no judgement" she stares at Jean hoping she understands

Jean nods "I know what you mean, I feel the same in my cab when driving down country roads, endless fields, and quaint cottages dotted around" she looks into Betty's eyes

"I bet you would love a cottage in the countryside wouldn't you" Betty says smiling leaning back feeling Jean's hand behind her shoulder

"Yes, it's my plan to buy a cottage in the country when this damn war is over, if it ever ends, sometimes I wonder can our boys get us there?" Jean replies with a sad look in her eyes

Betty moves a little closer now facing Jean, she rests her own hand on Jean's arm

"They will win this war, I feel it, we are delivering new

models of planes that are more up to the job, and we don't know what is going on behind closed doors" Betty gives a sympathetic look

Jean nods in agreement "You're right, our boys can do this" she cautiously moves closer sipping her wine

Betty places her wine on the side table, as she sits back again, she deliberately draws nearer to Jean, placing a hand on Jean's leg

Jean's breath hitches at the contact, she looks into Betty's blue eyes, flitting from one eye to the other

Betty now almost chest to chest "You know Jean, from the first day we met I have been extremely fond of you" she chuckles nervously "who else puts up with my singing in the truck"

Jean takes a deep intake of breath "Betty, I don't put up with anything, I adore your voice, it puts me at ease whilst driving... and when I see you, I feel a sense of calm and belonging"

Betty nods her head grinning "I know what you mean" she edges forward

Jean gets closer to Betty too, their lips just moments away

a moment of doubt crosses their minds, until Jean's gaze drops to Betty's lips

Betty no longer hesitates and moves in and closes the gap

between them, the taste of wine, a moan from Jean as the kiss deepens

Jean entwines her tongue with Betty's; she holds her glass of wine slightly away from them

Betty pulling on Jean's blazer not wanting to let go, her own breath becoming shallow

the kiss lingers, and then the feel of cold liquid between them

they pull away abruptly as Jean's wine lightly spills on them both

"Oh my god, I am so sorry Betty" Jean says feeling embarrassed and going red

Betty laughs heartedly "Don't worry it's an old dress… and that kiss was worth it"

Jean grins "It was pretty out of this world" she leans in stealing another brief kiss from soft lips

Betty melting at the touch of Jean's lips on hers once again, then picking up her glass of wine

they continue chatting and sipping wine, feeling a sense of calm with one another

but how can they love without anyone finding out, it's so unfair.

Inevitable Love

The rain comes down in a light drizzle outside the factory

Monique steps out of the building… she puts her umbrella up

close behind, Dottie comes bouncing out with excitement looking up to the sky

"Blimey Mon, this weather is a bit of sod, innit?" she chuckles

Monique holds her arm out for Dottie to link arms

"It certainly is mon trésor, that is why I have this" Monique gestures to the umbrella

Dottie laughs "Yeah Mon… always the sensible one aren't ya"

Monique's stomach flips to the sound of Dottie's laughter

"Oui, ma chérie… that I am" Monique says with a smirk

they walk towards the café for lunch, Dottie smiling as she can't help herself

Thank heavens for lunch time… especially with my Monique Dottie's thoughts consume her

Monique gives her the side eye and grins, her own thoughts come forth *Dottie you are so adorable and cute, sometimes it makes my heart melt.*

Moments later they arrive at the café, they both head inside, Monique holding the door

the scent of pie and liquor, and then the freshly made coffee engulfs their nostrils

the windows steamed up from cooking and an almost full café

and the sound of faint chatter from customers at nearby tables echo through the room

"Eh Mon, go grab that table over there will ya… I'll go get lunch yeah?" Dottie winks with a cheeky smile

Monique gazes at Dottie "Okay, but I buy next time" she quirks her eyebrows at Dottie meaning business

"Yeah, yeah… fair do's Mon… next time" Dottie grins relentlessly

"Give me your coat and I'll take it over to the table" Monique offers and holds her hand out

Dottie removes her coat and hands it to Monique "Fanks Mon… it's 'otter than a brothel in 'ere innit"

Monique takes the coat and laughs "I wouldn't know Dottie… I've never been to one before" she winks, turns and heads to the table.

Watching Dottie from a distance Monique's inner thoughts get the best of her *God, I love ma chérie Dottie*

Dottie chats away to the older woman behind the counter as she pays

waiting for the food to be plated, Dottie takes the opportunity and looks over at Monique… smiling and giving her a wave. Dottie's thoughts emerge *I love you Mon… so much it hurts* a slightly pained expression appears on her face

Dottie turns back and grabs the tray; she heads over to the table and places it down, before sitting opposite Monique

"Are you alright ma chérie?" Monique speaks with concern

Dottie looks up as she hands out the plates and cups of tea "I'm fine… it's nothing to worry 'bout Mon"

a silence adorns the table as they pick up knives and forks and start to eat their pie, mash and liquor

Monique understanding not to push Dottie. "Mmmm, this is delicious mon trésor" she pauses and looks at Dottie sincerely "thank you for treating me" she smiles widely

Dottie grins like the cat who got the cream "Absolute pleasure Mon… we should do it more often don'tcha fink?"

Monique nods in agreement "Oui, a weekly lunch out

together sounds necessary" she scrunches her nose with a slight smile forming on her lips

Dottie nods enthusiastically "Yeah… let's do it Mon."

They continue chatting about their morning and their week ahead

as they finish their meal, and drink the dregs of their tea, the time ticks by

Monique checks her watch "We should take a slow walk back"

Dottie nods and puts on her coat

they step out into the rain once again

Monique putting her umbrella up

Dottie links her arm through Monique's as they begin their walk back to the factory

they just make it across the road after a double-decker bus passes by, and the rain starts to come down heavily

"Oh god Mon, who turned the tap on full" Dottie grunts disapprovingly

Monique laughs and still thinks Dottie is cute, even when she is grumpy, she looks down one of the alleys "Down there… come on let's take shelter. It will most likely ease in a few minutes anyway" they briskly walk down the alleyway and slip into a deep wide commercial doorway for shelter

Monique tips the umbrella down in front of them to stop the rain pelting in on them

the distinct sound of the rain pattering on the umbrella, and the backsplash from the wet road as a nearby double-decker bus passes through a forming puddle

the smell of petrol fumes mixed with fresh rainfall fills the streets

Monique and Dottie laugh as they huddle closer together behind the umbrella to prevent getting wet and to keep warm

"Well, I'd never 'ave suggested lunch if I'd known it would rain cats and dogs" Dottie chuckles seemingly less disgruntled

"Ma chérie, I never understood that expression, and in any case, I also would not have declined lunch if I had known" Monique follows her words with a meaningful smile

Dottie gazes up at Monique

their eyes locked on one another, Monique's eyes fall to Dottie's lips momentarily

God, I wanna kiss 'er so bad Dottie thinks to herself, and before she can stop herself, her lips are on Monique's in a brief kiss before she abruptly pulls away the expression on Monique's face panics Dottie

Monique's heart is racing, her eyes widen, her stomach doing somersaults, then her silence is interrupted by a quivering voice

"Oh god, Monique… I-I'm sorry" Dottie's eyes fill with unshed tears, a guilt-ridden tone in her voice, she unhooks her arm and steps down off the doorway step

Monique not wanting to lose this opportunity, grabs Dottie's arm and pulls her back onto the step

they stare at one another, words unspoken

Dottie's face red with embarrassment for overstepping the boundaries

without warning Monique leans down taking Dottie's lips to hers

as they embrace in a sensual, deepening kiss… Monique lets out a soft moan, feeling a pulsating sensation between her legs

Dottie's tongue slides between their lips and entwines with Monique's, her own heart racing, heat rushing through her core

then as the rain begins to ease, they reluctantly pull away from one another

Monique speaks softly and quietly "Don't apologise ma

chérie… I have wanted this since the first day we met"

Dottie now trembling, her confidence and bravery pushed back… she speaks with quivering tone "I thought I did wrong Mon" her tears spilling over uncontrollably

Monique gives her a sympathetic smile, wiping away tears with the pad of her thumb "Never mon trésor… you see things in Paris are more open, if you understand me. Being in England is much harder to read"

Dottie exhales in a sigh of relief and Monique gives her a reassuring smile

"I love you Mon… I'm not afraid of sayin' it, and I know what ya mean" Dottie replies with a confident but unexpecting tone

Monique grins as the words penetrate her ears "Je t'aime aussi… ma chérie Dottie."

With all that is said and done they both step down off the doorway step and continue walking back to the factory

in comfortable silence, and a newfound relief of being open with each other.

Coming Home

Olive sits upon the weathered wooden memorial bench,
gazing out across the calm lake

her family allowing her a moment alone with her
memories

now aged ninety-four, and remembering her meaningful
work here all those years ago

it was the early forties… however, it is not the work she
remembers the most

she recalls the secret moments shared, with the one she
loves so dearly

"Oh, Elizabeth" she murmurs quietly with sadness

the woman she truly loves, deep in her heart, and deep in
her soul

she smiles as she recalls their life together, although they
parted after the war

they briefly reunited in nineteen sixty-four, for a special
trip to Paris… a trip she thought would be the very last
time for them to be together

until nineteen ninety-two when tragedy brought them
together once again… and this time for good

her eyes gently close, followed by a deep intake of breath

she is back in that time of nineteen forty-four, with the love of her life

Olive can feel Elizabeth's pinkie finger clasped with hers

recalling their quiet conversations, sharing a sandwich together on this very bench

she can still taste the luxury of the egg and cress, and hear the rustling of the wax paper

then she feels Elizabeth's lips on her cheek, from those stolen lunch break kisses

a smile adorns Olive's face at the beautiful memory

followed by the subtle scent of the distinct musty smell from the huts… where she once spent her working hours

and with that, she takes her last breath in this life.

Then there she is… her one true love

Elizabeth links her pinkie finger once again with hers and she speaks softly

"I've been waiting for you, Olive!" followed by a wide smile

her short blonde bouncy curls are the same as they were

back then when they met

Olive returns the smile, noticing Elizabeth is wearing her WREN's uniform

as she replies with tears in her eyes "Oh, Elizabeth… I have missed you every day of my living life without you"

and Olive… now her younger self, and wearing her favourite outfit of the time, a plain brown dress, finished with a worn leather belt

as they stand and begin to stroll the lake gravel path one last time

the unspoken words are what speaks the loudest

for they have now 'come home' to each other… for all eternity.

L oryh brx

Caesar Cipher —shift 3

www.ingramcontent.com/pod-product-compliance
Lightning Source LLC
LaVergne TN
LVHW051020080826
845145LV00009B/2723

* 9 7 8 1 0 3 6 9 5 0 7 6 7 *